# THE SMURF MENACE

*Peyo*

# WITHDRAWN

# THE SMURF MENACE

Smurf them here and untie them! I'll smurf the Great Leader!

Gulp!

A **SMURFS** GRAPHIC NOVEL BY *Peyo*

WITH THE COLLABORATION OF
LUC PARTHOENS AND THIERRY CULLIFORD — SCRIPT
ALAIN MAURY AND LUC PARTHOENS — ARTWORK
NINE — COLOR

PAPERCUTZ™
NEW YORK

# SMURFS GRAPHIC NOVELS AVAILABLE FROM PAPERCUTZ ™

THE SMURFS graphic novels are available in paperback for $5.99 each and in hardcover for $10.99 each, except for THE SMURFS #21 and #22, which are $7.99 in paperback and $12.99 in hardcover, at booksellers everywhere. You can also order online at papercutz.com. Or call 1-800-886-1223, Monday through Friday, 9 – 5 EST. MC, Visa, and AmEx accepted. To order by mail, please add $4.00 for postage and handling for first book ordered, $1.00 for each additional book and make check payable to NBM Publishing. Send to: Papercutz, 160 Broadway, Suite 700, East Wing, New York, NY 10038.

THE SMURFS graphic novels are also available digitally wherever e-books are sold.

PAPERCUTZ.COM

**THE SMURF MENACE** © Peyo - 2017 - Licensed through Lafig Belgium - www.smurf.com

*English translation copyright © 2017 by Papercutz.*
*All rights reserved.*

"The Smurf Menace"
BY PEYO
WITH THE COLLABORATION OF
LUC PARTHOENS AND THIERRY CULLIFORD FOR THE SCRIPT,
ALAIN MAURY AND LUC PARTHOENS FOR ARTWORK,
NINE FOR COLORS.

"The Shadow of the Smurf Apprentice"
BY PEYO

"The Mansion of a Thousand Mirrors"
BY PEYO

Joe Johnson, SMURFLATIONS
Adam Grano, SMURFIC DESIGN
Janice Chiang, LETTERING SMURFETTE
Matt. Murray, SMURF CONSULTANT
Rachel Pinnelas, SMURF COORDINATOR
Jeff Whitman, ASSISTANT MANAGING SMURF
Jim Salicrup, SMURF-IN-CHIEF

PAPERBACK EDITION ISBN: 978-1-62991-622-4
HARDCOVER EDITION ISBN: 978-1-62991-623-1

PRINTED IN CHINA JANUARY 2017 BY WKT CO. LTD.

Papercutz books may be purchased for business or promotional use. For information on bulk purchases please contact Macmillan Corporate and Premium Sales Department at (800) 221-7945 x5442.

DISTRIBUTED BY MACMILLAN
FIRST PAPERCUTZ PRINTING

You all know the Smurfs, those little blue elves who live in the heart of an impenetrable forest...

Ready jokesters and bon vivants...

Hee hee hee! I really smurfed you!

?

Hefty Smurf, I wonder how you can still get smurfed by Jokey Smurf's pranks!

!

Oh, come on! We know how he is! An occasional practical joke won't smurf anyone any harm!

Meanwhile, that won't smurf my sacks!

...and who selflessly help one another...

Hold on! I'll smurf you a hand!

Me, too!

Thanks, my friends!

In short, the Smurfs live in perfect harmony.

"Used to live," we should say because, for some time now, go figure, things have changed...

Hey!

You should watch where you're smurfing!

It's your fault, you stupid smurf!

© Peyo [1]

Could you smurf me a hand?

What now? I have something else to smurf!

?

Hey, you! Don't you have anything else to smurf besides playing ball?

Oh! Whatever! Leave us smurf!

That Jokey Smurf is seriously starting to get on my smurfs!

♪ Pfff! ♪ With this heat, that's the fourth time already I've had to smurf water from the well today! That Lazy Smurf won't be the one to help me!

That's right! It's always the same ones who work and the same ones who don't smurf anything in this village!

Ah! There you are, Handy Smurf! I was looking for you!

?

It's been two days since you promised to smurf my shutters, and I'm still waiting!

Well then, you can just go smurf your shutters yourself. Here!

!

2

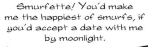
Smurfette! You'd make me the happiest of smurfs, if you'd accept a date with me by moonlight.

With you? No way! Have you ever really smurfed at yourself?

⌐Pff!⌐ Just who does she smurf she is?

Hey, Vanity Smurf! I found the mirror I'd smurfed from you!

Oh, thanks, Jokey Smurf! I'll be able to admire myself again!

AAAH!

Hee, hee, hee! It was a trick mirror!

⌐WAAAAAH!⌐ I'm ugly!

Jokey Smurf! Aren't you ashamed? Look what you've smurfed!

⌐Sniff!⌐

Nah! It's his own fault! He shouldn't be so sensitive!

And anyhow, it's true that he's smurfily ugly!

What's going on with the Smurfs? They're ordinarily so kind, I no longer recognize them! I'll have to talk to them to set things smurf!

© Peyo 3

7

Soon after...

My little Smurfs, I am smurfly unhappy with you! For some time now, you keep squabbling with each other!

I know! It's not easy to always smurf on your smurf behavior and to put up with others' faults every day.

But believe me! If you continue like this, our village's unity is endangered! Now, go and think about what I've just smurfed to you!

Bravo, Papa Smurf! A superb speech, too! I'm sure they've smurfed your message!

Let's hope!

CLAP CLAP

What's Papa Smurf talking about? We don't argue!

No way!

It'd be like you getting mad at me about that hammer I smurfed from you the other day and still haven't returned!

That's right! You could resmurf it to me, you know!

Nah! It's just a hammer, after all!

Yes, but it's MY hammer!

Oh, all right! For smurf's sake!

THIEF!

Take that back, or else—

4

*Alas, far from disappearing, the discord among the Smurfs only increased in subsequent days...*

Careful! I mustn't smurf a single drop!

What?! What's all that racket?

You get on my smurfs with your music!

You hick!

That's enough! Aren't you ashamed?

He's the one who started it, Papa Smurf!

That's not even true! And for starters, it's Chef Smurf's fault, he's the one who--

**ENOUGH! ENOUGH!**

I don't want to hear it! Go home and stay there!

This isn't smurf!

We'll see who gets the last smurf!

They haven't understood a thing!

How can I get them to understand they're smurfing straight for a disaster?!

Hmmm... I have a little idea that'll smurf them a good lesson!

*What mysterious idea is taking seed in Papa Smurf's mind?*

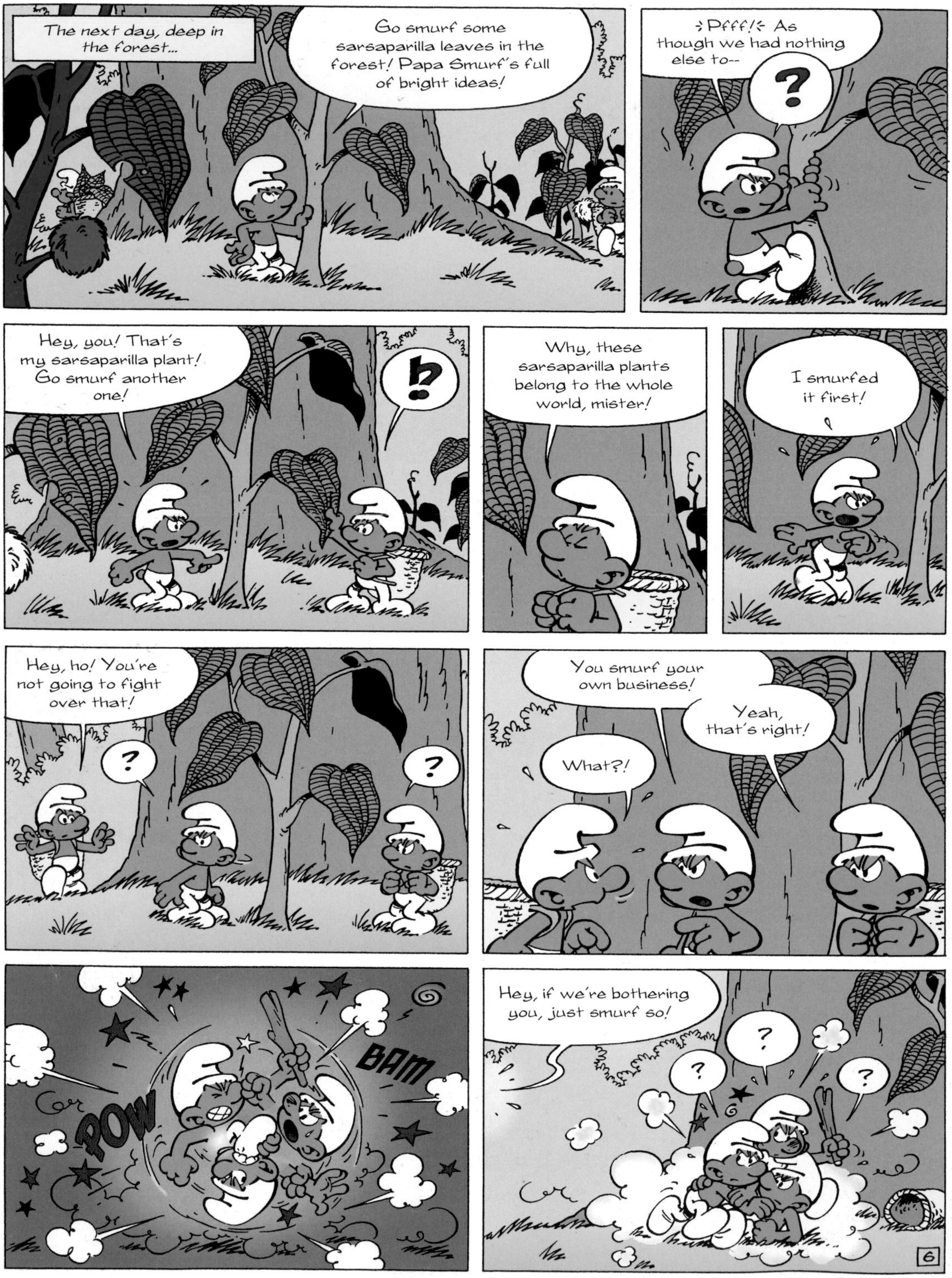

The next day, deep in the forest...
Go smurf some sarsaparilla leaves in the forest! Papa Smurf's full of bright ideas!
Pfff! As though we had nothing else to--
?
Hey, you! That's my sarsaparilla plant! Go smurf another one!
!?
Why, these sarsaparilla plants belong to the whole world, mister!
I smurfed it first!
Hey, ho! You're not going to fight over that!
?
?
You smurf your own business!
Yeah, that's right!
What?!
BAM
POW
Hey, if we're bothering you, just smurf so!
?
?
?
6

Go ahead! We wouldn't want to smurf you!

Who are you?

Where did you smurf from? We've never seen you around here!

Are you Smurfs?

It doesn't matter. Can you tell us why you're smurfing in our sarsaparilla field?

What do you mean YOUR sarsaparilla field?

Exactly! This field is the property of our village, and it seems to me you're smurfing here without authorization!

These sarsaparilla fields are ours!

We'll see about that! Go ahead, fellows! Smurf those thieves for me!

Huh?!

There's too many of them! I have to run and warn the others!

Hey! One's smurfing away!

Bah, too bad! Smurf those two! We'll take them to the Great Leader!

They're--they're smurfing them with them! Who can they be?

I can't abandon my friends like this! I'll follow them!

I'd better not get smurfed!

But where are they smurfing them?

Oh! My goodness! !?

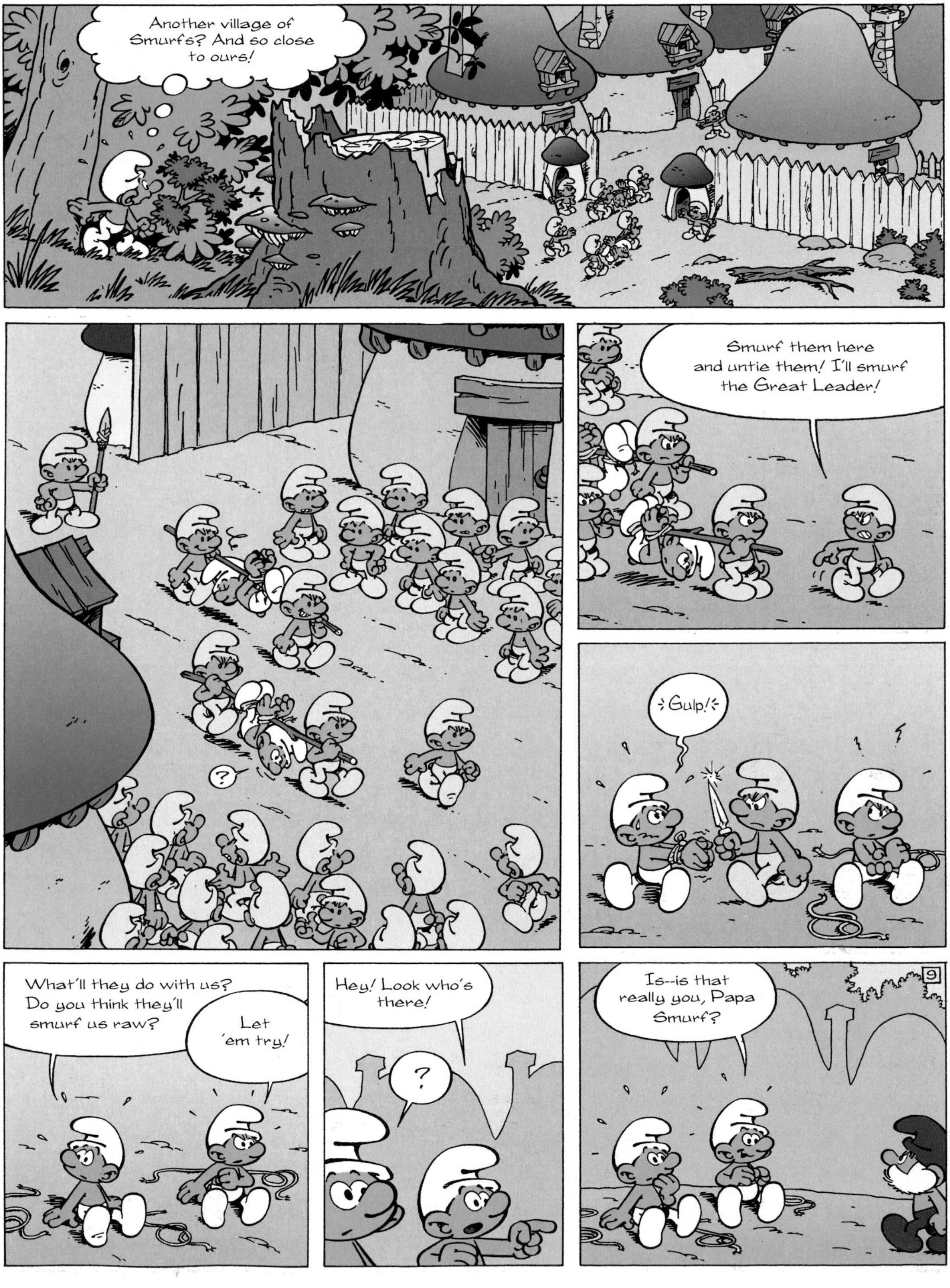
Another village of Smurfs? And so close to ours!
Smurf them here and untie them! I'll smurf the Great Leader!
Gulp!
What'll they do with us? Do you think they'll smurf us raw?
Let 'em try!
Hey! Look who's there!
?
Is--is that really you, Papa Smurf?

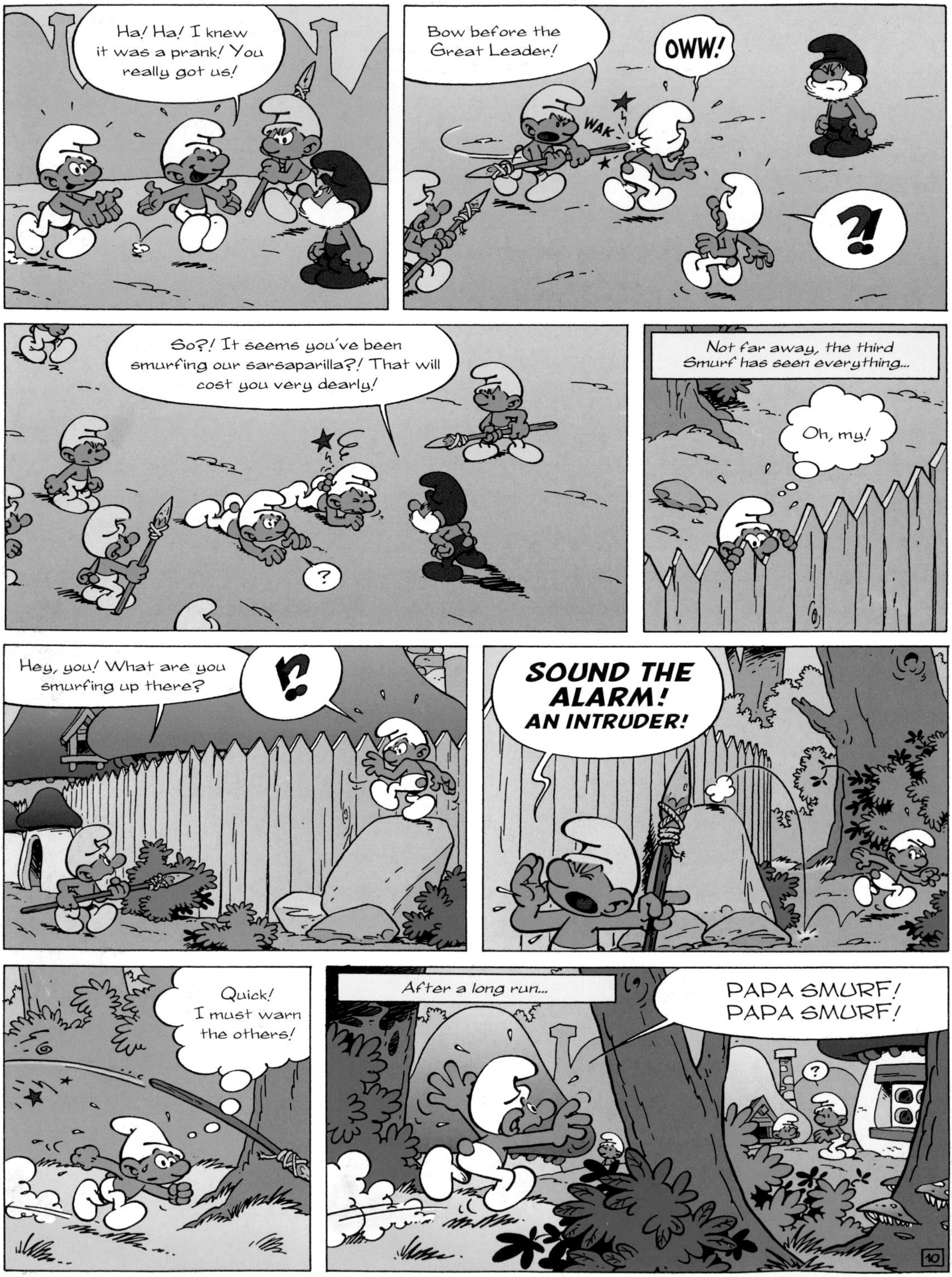
Ha! Ha! I knew it was a prank! You really got us!
Bow before the Great Leader!
OWW!
WAK
?!
So?! It seems you've been smurfing our sarsaparilla?! That will cost you very dearly!
?
Not far away, the third Smurf has seen everything...
Oh, my!
Hey, you! What are you smurfing up there?
!?
SOUND THE ALARM! AN INTRUDER!
Quick! I must warn the others!
After a long run...
PAPA SMURF! PAPA SMURF!
?
10

Papa Smurf! It's a catasmurfre!

What's going on?

We were just having a little argument... um...smurfing sarsaparilla when they arrived. So, they attacked us, then they smurfed the other two to their village, and then you came... Well, the other Papa Smurf, and then he gave him a pop on the smurf, and then the guard arrived who smurfed me with his spear and then I smurfed away....

Wait! What are you smurfing us? Who's "they"?

The others... the other Smurfs!

The other Smurfs?!

Come now! You know full well we're the only Smurfs!

If you don't believe me, follow me, I'll smurf you!

Well, let's go, since he's asking us to smurf him!

Shortly after...

Have you seen those intruders?

Yes! Two of them are locked up, but the third one ran away! That's why we have to smurf rounds in the vicinity of the village! The Great Leader thinks he'll come back with his friends!

I'm sure with the fright that he got, we won't be smurfing him any time soon!

HA! HA! HA! That's smurfing right!

15

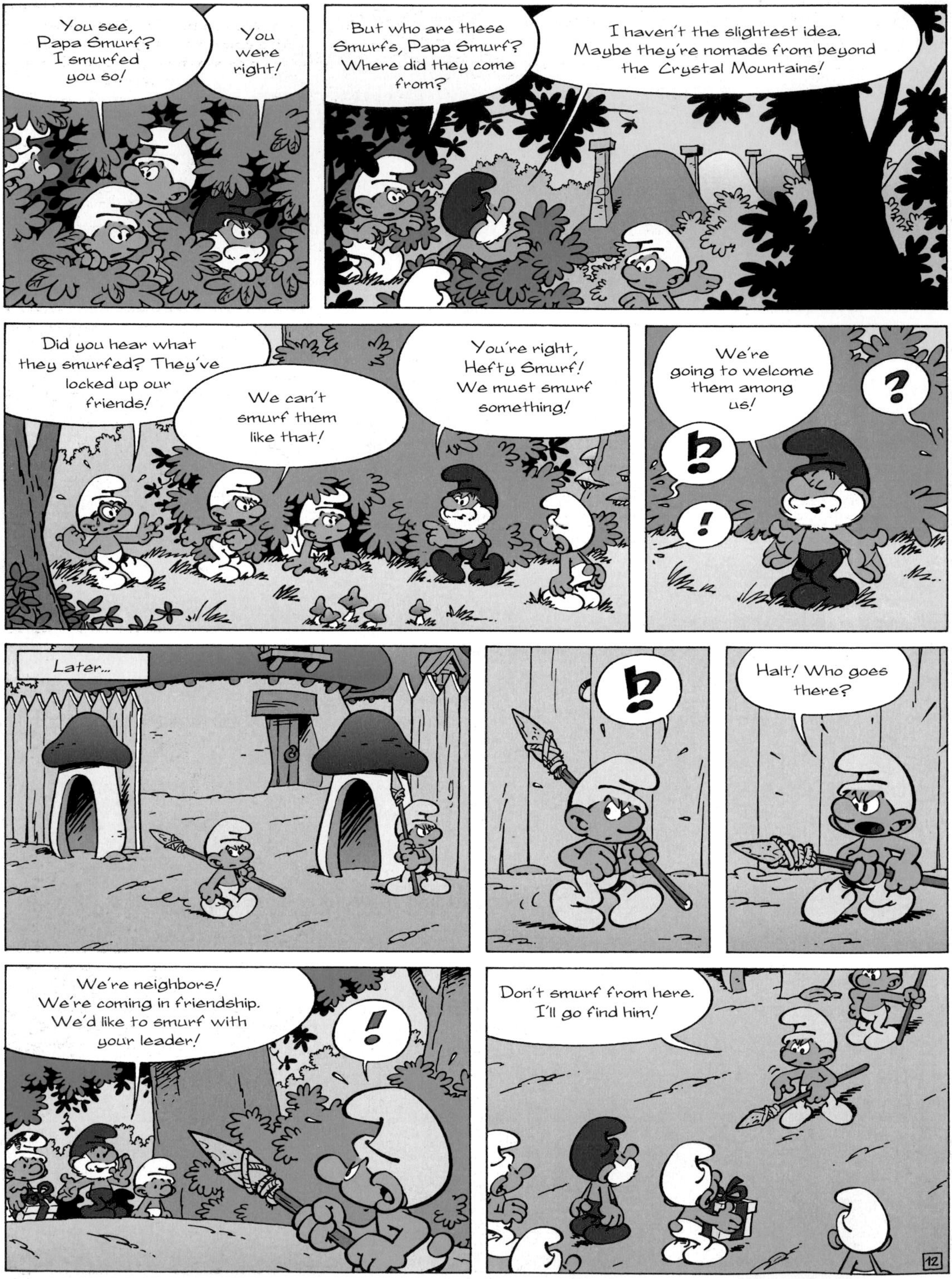

You see, Papa Smurf? I smurfed you so!
You were right!
But who are these Smurfs, Papa Smurf? Where did they come from?
I haven't the slightest idea. Maybe they're nomads from beyond the Crystal Mountains!
Did you hear what they smurfed? They've locked up our friends!
We can't smurf them like that!
You're right, Hefty Smurf! We must smurf something!
We're going to welcome them among us!
?
!?
!
Later...
!?
Halt! Who goes there?
We're neighbors! We're coming in friendship. We'd like to smurf with your leader!
!
Don't smurf from here. I'll go find him!
12

What do you want?

We live not far from here! We came to ask you to free our friends whom you smurfed by mistake...

By mistake?... But they're thieves! They smurfed our sarsaparilla!

That sarsaparilla is everyone's! Anybody can smurf it!

Well, since we're here, that's no longer true! Now it's ours!

You said: "since we're here." Where, in fact, did you smurf from?

From very far away! Anyhow, it's none of your business!

Really? In any case, we came to smurf you a few presents as a gesture of welcome!

You want to purchase your friends' freedom? Do you think a few trinkets will make me change my mind?

It's a sign of a good leader to be able to be magnanimous!

13

Hmm!... It's all right this time! But we'd better not smurf them there again, or else...

Go smurf the prisoners!

Papa Smurf?! **YIPPEEEE!**

Hefty Smurf, Jokey Smurf! You're here, too!

We'll smurf a little party among friends tomorrow evening! Would you do us the pleasure of coming?

A party?! Why that's decadent! Certainly not!

Oh?! Okay! Too bad! Let's go home, Smurfs!

Those Smurfs don't inspire much confidence in me!

Come, come, Hefty Smurf! They're a little strange, that's all!

The next evening, at the party, the newcomers are the topic of all conversations...

Papa Smurf! Look!

14

You came?! I'm happy you smurfed your minds!

I smurf my mind whenever I want to!

Of course... but I see that you've brought along a lady-smurf.

Welcome to the Smurf Village!

!

Um... well, my friends, we have guests. Let's give them a warm welcome.

Yum... heh, heh! You look like a food lover, too! Here, smurf a piece of cake...But leave some for the others! Yum!...

No! It's all mine!

?

YUM!
SLURP
CRUNCH

But--

?!

I'm still hungry!

Hey! Why are you smurfing at my piece of cake like that?

15

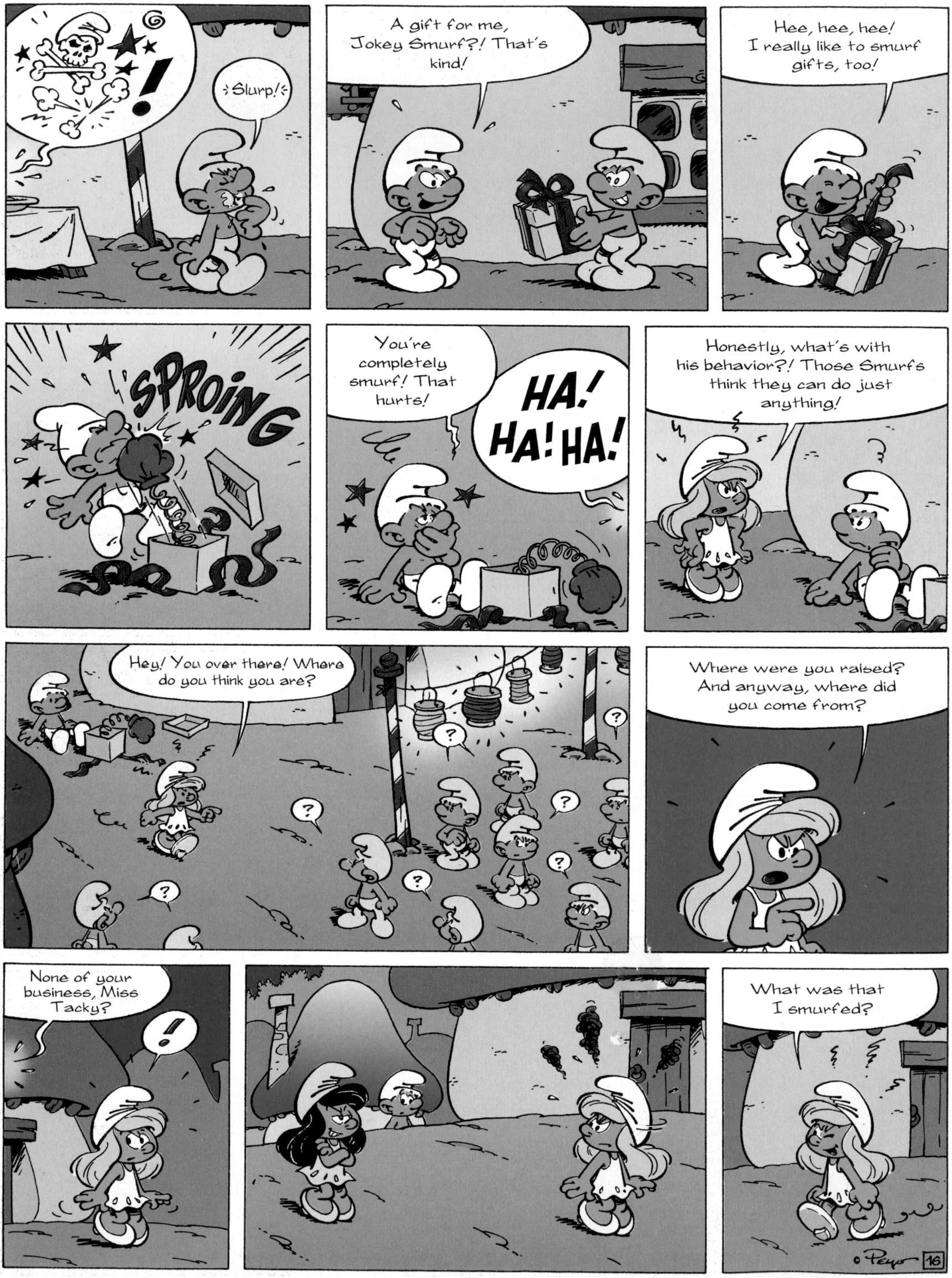
Slurp!
A gift for me, Jokey Smurf?! That's kind!
Hee, hee, hee! I really like to smurf gifts, too!
SPROING
You're completely smurf! That hurts!
HA! HA! HA!
Honestly, what's with his behavior?! Those Smurfs think they can do just anything!
Hey! You over there! Where do you think you are?
Where were you raised? And anyway, where did you come from?
None of your business, Miss Tacky?
What was that I smurfed?
Peyo
16

The truth smurfs, dearie!

SLOB! SHREW! FAKE BLONDE!

YOU COW! WITCH! YOU SNAKE!

Come now! Let's smurf our calm!

Uh... hmm... anyways, I think it's time to go to bed! Tomorrow, we must smurf repairs to the dam!

You have a dam? Where?

Near the lake! Why?

No reason! Come, my dear, I think there's nothing else for us to smurf here!

∻Pff!∻ You shouldn't have stepped in, Papa Smurf! I'd have made mashed smurf with her!

The next day...

∻Pff!∻ I'm going to smurf the dam!

Be quiet or I'll tell Papa Smurf!

Oh! Papa Smurf! Look!

?

Well, I never! You see that?! What are those Smurfs smurfing to our dam?

They're smurfing it up! Such a beautiful piece of work!

By my word as Hefty Smurf, they won't smurf away with this Let's go smurf them a piece of our minds!

Wait!

Yeah! Let's go!

You're right! Hey, over there! That's our dam!

Heh, heh, heh!

~Pff...

18

Papa Smurf! They're smurfing a canal to take part of our water!

Is that true?

Exactly! We need water, too, to smurf our crops! Do you have any objection to that?

No! It's an excellent idea! We'll even help you smurf the work!

No way, Papa Smurf! Surely we're not going to help them smurf our own dam?!

There's no way I am!

I'm sure it's because you're incapable of smurfing such a job!

Smurf that again, if you dare!

Hefty Smurf! No!

BZZZZZZZ

We'll see who can't smurf the job! Get to work!

Soon after...

You see, we smurfed part of those logs there to smurf them here and open a new canal!

19

But the structure is smurfily weakened!

Ha! Ha! Ha! What are you smurfing about? You're the one to be teaching me my job!

Look at that beam! It's not holding! It's dangerous!

Bah! Two nails, and nobody will smurf a thing!

BAM BAM

That's badly smurfed work! I'm sure Papa Smurf and your Leader won't agree!

The Leader? Once it's done, he couldn't smurf less! And your Papa Smurf, ⸘pfiiiit!⸘

!

Meanwhile...

My favorite thing is telling on others! Follow me, you'll see!

?

Him, for example, I'll smurf him in the act! Heh heh!

ZZZ

Ahaaa! Caught in the smurf! I'll tell the Great Leader, and that'll cost you three whacks with the stick!

Elsewhere...

Once we've finished smurfing this hole, we'll have to smurf the pole.

⸘Yawwwn!⸘ That's it, a little more effort. We're almost there!

20

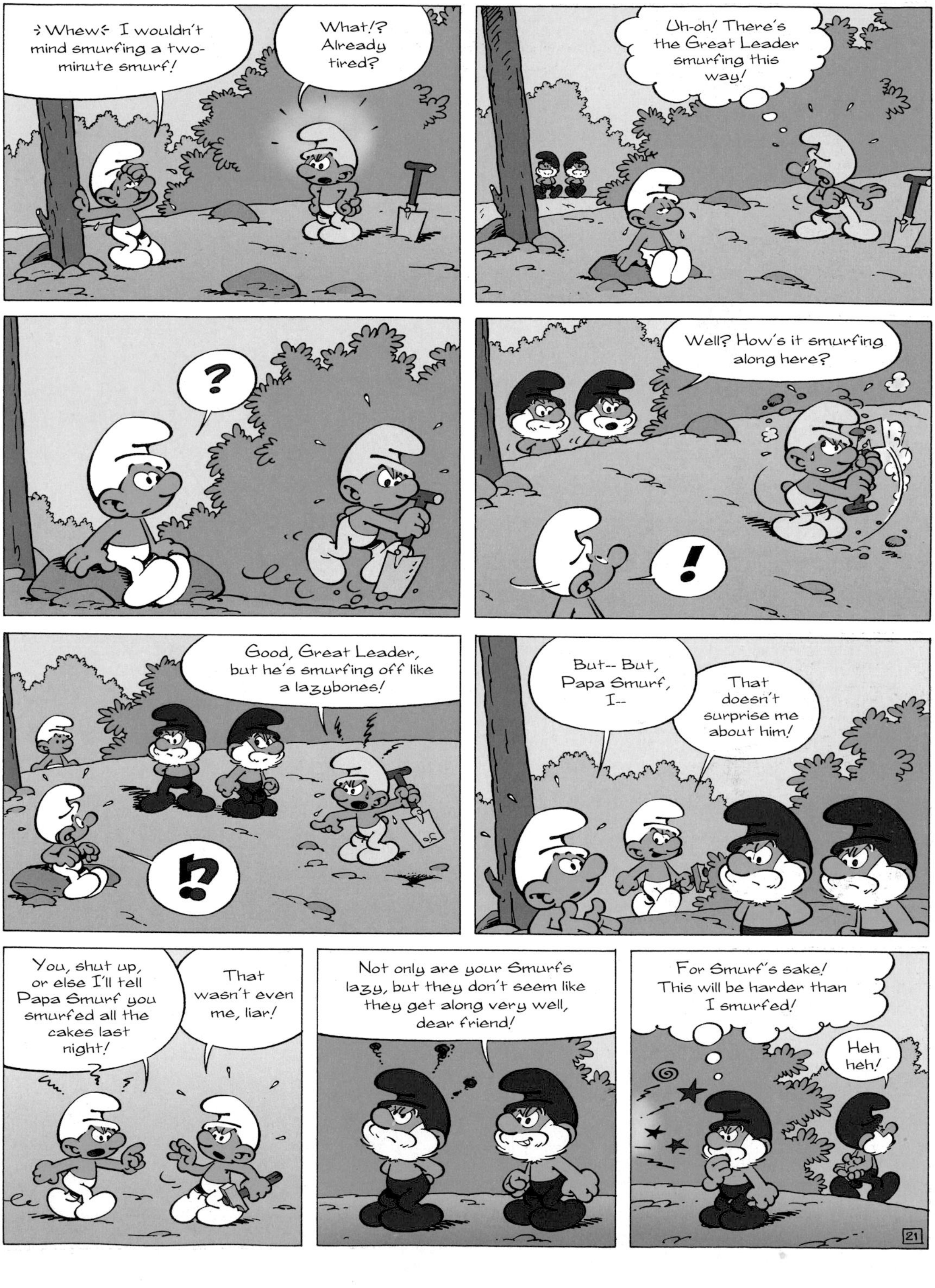

-:- Whew -:- I wouldn't mind smurfing a two-minute smurf!
What!? Already tired?
Uh-oh! There's the Great Leader smurfing this way!
?
Well? How's it smurfing along here?
!
Good, Great Leader, but he's smurfing off like a lazybones!
But-- But, Papa Smurf, I--
That doesn't surprise me about him!
You, shut up, or else I'll tell Papa Smurf you smurfed all the cakes last night!
That wasn't even me, liar!
Not only are your Smurfs lazy, but they don't seem like they get along very well, dear friend!
For Smurf's sake! This will be harder than I smurfed!
Heh heh!
21

After a hard day's work...

I don't understand why Papa Smurf accepts working with those Smurfs!

For once, I agree with you, Hefty Smurf!

Well, I don't agree! I think they're very interesting, especially the one with glasses!

Thanks to him, they obey perfectly, because he keeps watch and reports all the cheaters to the Great Leader, who punishes them severely. What's more, I think we should smurf the same thing, too...

Would you smurf this for me, please?

Of course!

And then, in any case, if Papa Smurf says we have to work with them, there's no smurfing about it, because--

POW

Thanks!

My pleasure!

I'll tell Papa Smurf!

Morning...

Hey! Where are you off to, Hefty Smurf?

To the river! I'm going to smurf my morning exercises!

May I come with you?

Okay, but you'd better not smurf the slightest prank on me, or else...

22

Oooh! Bravo!

CLAP CLAP

?!

!

SPLÁT

Jokey Smurf! You blithering smurf! You smurfed all the water from the river!

But-- But--

But it's impossible for him to have smurfed all the water! This isn't normal!

We've got to tell Papa Smurf!

?

A few moments later...

What? The river is dry?

Papa Smurf! My plant beds are no longer being irrigated!

Quick! To the dam!

At the dam...

**?!**

The Great Leader was right, there they are! Careful, smurf up the ranks!

**HALT!** Why have you come smurfing here?

Our village no longer has any water!

Orders of the Great Leader! We need a lot of water for our crops!

We have crops to smurf, too, for Smurf's sake!

Orders are orders! There's no smurfing about it!

It's not fair! That's our dam!

Yeah!

That's right!

We won't let ourselves be smurfed around!

Correction: it <u>was</u> your dam! Since the transformations, it's ours!

And enough smurfing! Attack! Let's chase 'em away!

**?!**

**CHARGE!**

Run away, my little Smurfs!

OWW!

No, mercy!

Heh heh heh!

YEEOWWW!

?

Farmer Smurf! You smurfed my life!

It was my pleasure!

Later, in the forest...

All right! I think we've lost them!

And what'll we smurf now, Papa Smurf?

Let's do like them! Let's smurf some weapons, attack them, and smurf them a lesson!

Weapons? Certainly not, Hefty Smurf! Do you really want us to become like them?

You're no doubt right, Papa Smurf! But it is our dam, after all!

We'll smurf a solution in the coming days! Now, let's return to the village!

25

29

The following days, the situation only gets worse...

Smurf it all to smurf! Without the water from the dam, my vegetables won't last long! If this continues, we won't have anything left to smurf!

Luckily, there are the others coming back from gathering food!

Hey, it looks like something's going on!

--and there were three Gray Smurfs near the bridge--

They made us smurf our whole harvest to them to be able to come back to the village!

There were only three, and you didn't smurf anything to stop them?!

It's just...⸘gulp⸘ they had their weapons, Hefty Smurf...

Bah! You're nothing but wimps!

I've had it with those Smurfs! For starters, they smurf our plant beds, then our dam, and now our harvest!

Maybe you want to be taken adsmurfed of, not me!

So, who wants to come with me to smurf back what's ours?

Okay, I get it. I'll go alone!

26

Papa Smurf says we mustn't smurf violence with violence, and that--

POW

We can't let him smurf by himself! I'm following him!...

Me, too!

A few moments later, near the bridge...

Heh heh heh! We don't even have to pick fruit anymore! Those stupid Smurfs'll do it for us!

Yeah! Soon those simpletons will be our servants!

CHOMP CHOMP

Especially the one with the little heart tattoo! That one makes me laugh! WHA-HA-HA!

The "little heart" has just two words to smurf to you, you stupid smurf!

?

!

?!

Uh-oh! I can't watch! He's going to get smurfed!

BIF BAM SOK

?!?

27

That's right! Run away, you cowards!

You'll get what's smurfing to you! We'll be seeing you!

OWWWW OWW!

YEAAAAAH!

Hurray for Hefty Smurf!

Later, in Smurf Village...

I did remind him what you'd said, but he smurfed me a smack on the smurf and then he went to smurf the Gray Smurfs!...

?

It's Hefty Smurf! It seems he gave them a smurfing!

HIP HIP HURRAY!

You disobeyed me, Hefty Smurf!

Well...let's just say... that...

Well, yes! I disobeyed. But we couldn't let those Smurfs go on smurfing from us all our belongings. They deserved a good lesson!

You can't punish him, Papa Smurf! He smurfed the village's honor!

And also, those Smurfs are hypocritical and selfish! They never smurf anything for others!

28

I'd told you, however, to not resmurf to violence with violence! Next time, don't you disobey again!

But-- But--⁉

YEAAAAH!

HURRAY FOR HEFTY SMURF!

HURRAY FOR PAPA SMURF!

I didn't think this could happen! It's nice to see them like before again!

YAY!

PAPA SMURF! PAPA SMURF!

?

Papa Smurf, I have a message for you from the Gray Smurfs!

A message? Where is it?

Here!

!

?

What is it, Papa Smurf?

An ultimatum: "One of yours cowardly smurfed three of us when they were unarmed! Hand him over or else."

Well, I never--! Who do those Gray Smurfs think they are?

Let them come smurf him, if they dare!

I don't feel good at all about this turn of events! It may be time to stop everything!

We'll never hand Hefty Smurf over to them, will we, Papa Smurf?!

29

Of course not!

!

THWACK

THEN IT'S WAR!

Look!

?!

?

You, climb atop the tower and smurf me what you see!

Right away, Papa Smurf!

A few moments later...

They're everywhere! The village is surrounded!

They're armed to the smurfs! They even have things--You know, machines.

Machines?...

?

?!

Why yes, you know-- To smurf stones!

FIRE!

To smurf stones?

BOOOM

Catapults!

Catapults!

That's it! Catapults!

30

34

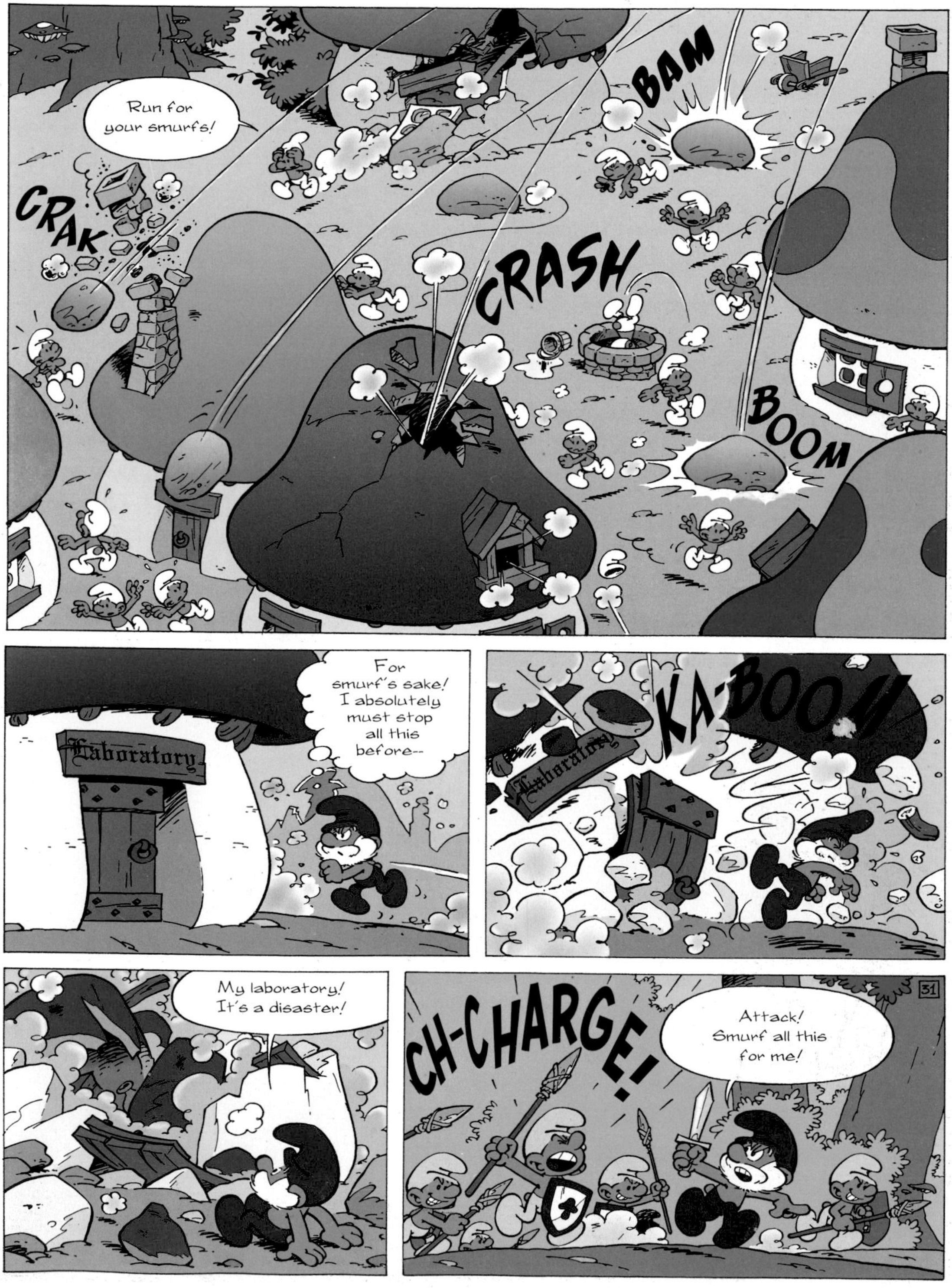
Run for your smurfs!
CRAK
BAM
CRASH
BOOM
Laboratory
For smurf's sake! I absolutely must stop all this before--
KA-BOOM!!
Laboratory
My laboratory! It's a disaster!
31
CH-CHARGE!
Attack! Smurf all this for me!

For the poor, unarmed Smurfs, the fight is unequal and gives them... the attackers' advantage...

These catapults aren't bad, eh? It's my latest invention.

Bah! I'm sure it must be smurfly heavy and cumbersome!

Cumbersome? What do you think of this one, then?

OWW!

BOP

SHWING

I'll tell Papa Smurf!

Me, too!

Heh heh heh! So, Mister Hefty, not so tough now?

I absolutely must resmurf that grimoire, or this could mean the end of the village.

There it is! Thank Smurfness, it's intact!

May we ask the reason for your enthusiasm?

?

32

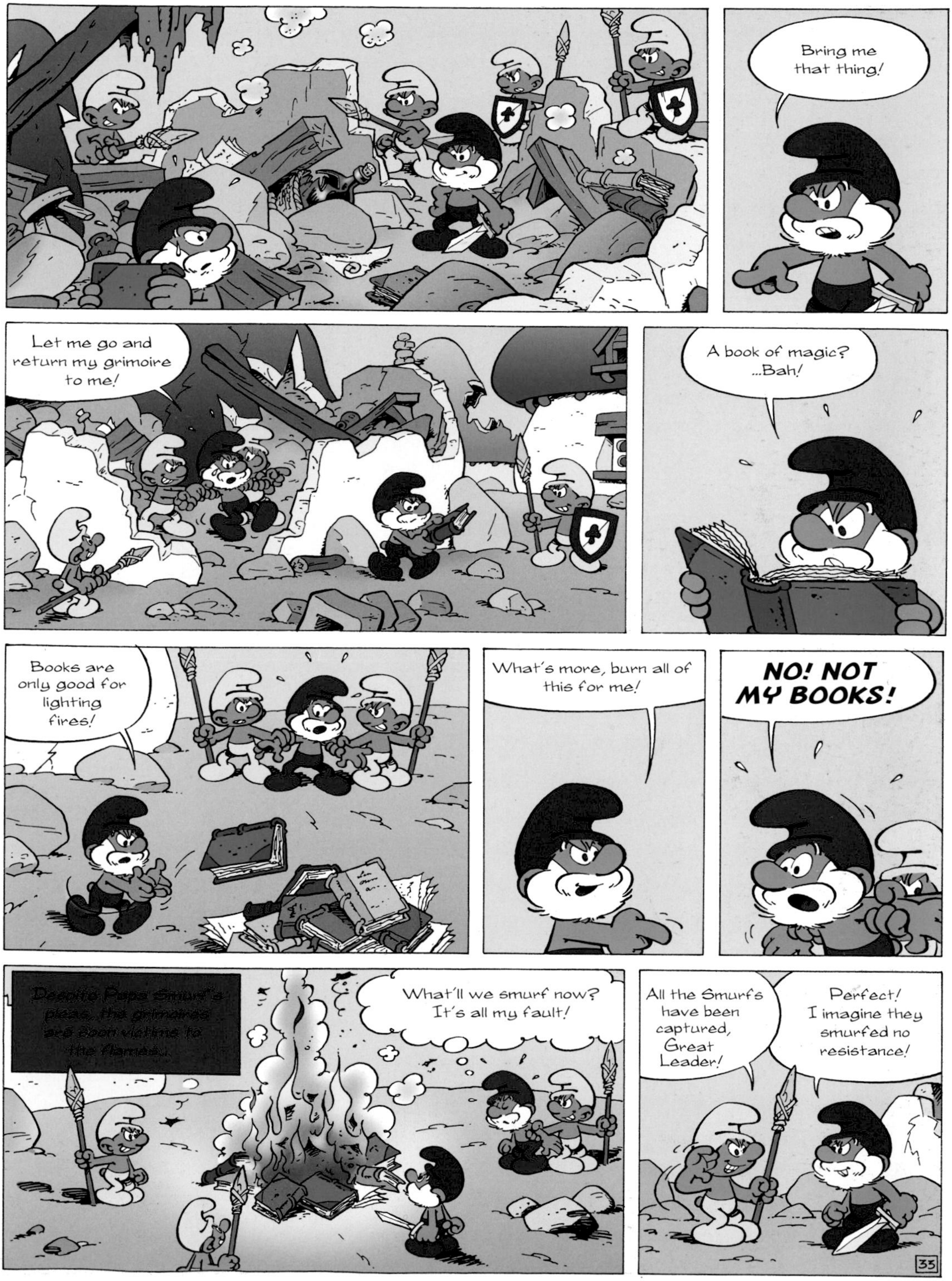
Bring me that thing!
Let me go and return my grimoire to me!
A book of magic? ...Bah!
Books are only good for lighting fires!
What's more, burn all of this for me!
NO! NOT MY BOOKS!
Despite Papa Smurf's pleas, the grimoires are soon victims to the flames...
What'll we smurf now? It's all my fault!
All the Smurfs have been captured, Great Leader!
Perfect! I imagine they smurfed no resistance!
33

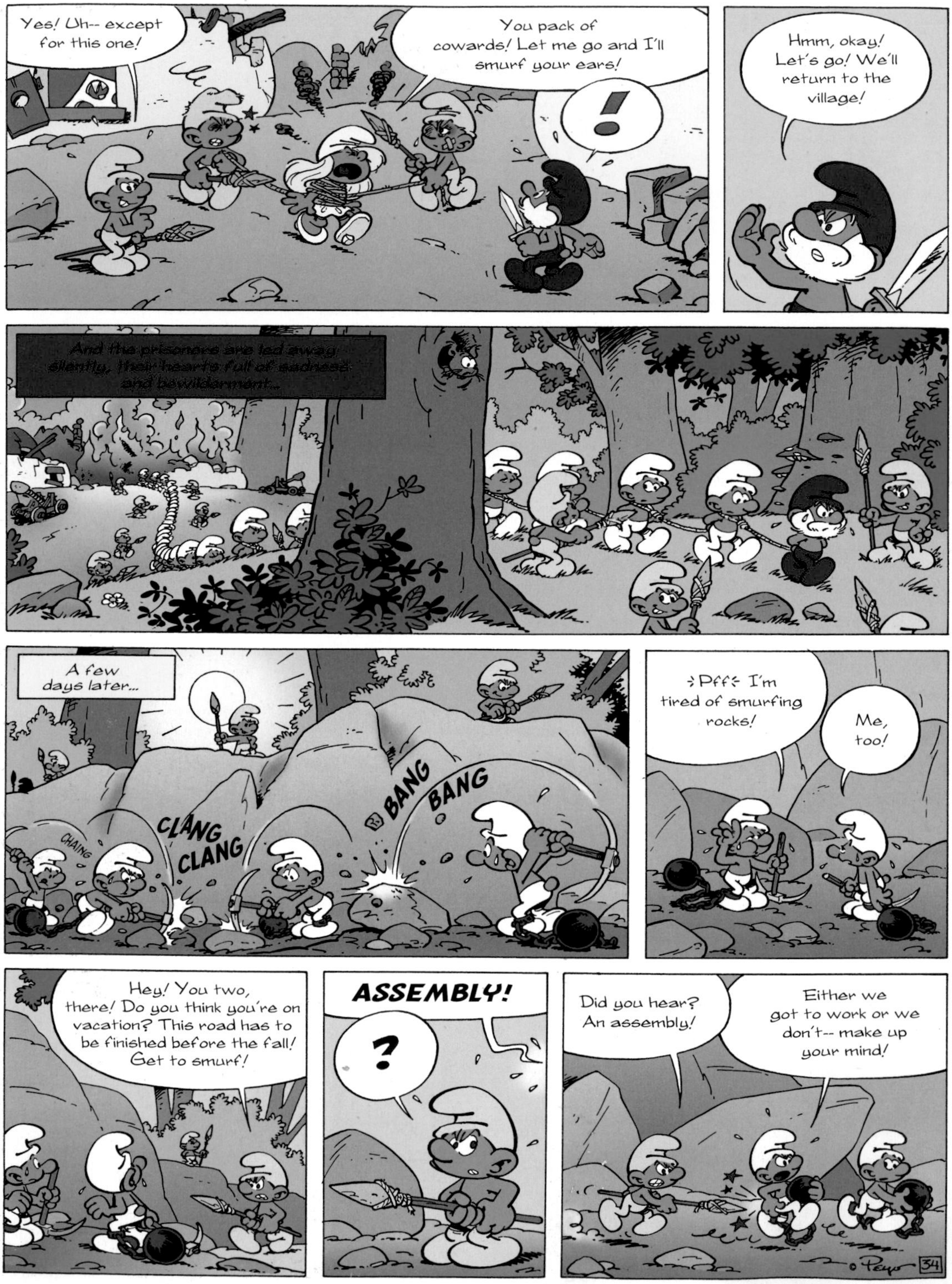
Yes! Uh-- except for this one!
You pack of cowards! Let me go and I'll smurf your ears!
!
Hmm, okay! Let's go! We'll return to the village!
And the prisoners are led away silently, their hearts full of sadness and bewilderment...
A few days later...
CHAING
CLANG
CLANG
BANG
BANG
Pff I'm tired of smurfing rocks!
Me, too!
Hey! You two, there! Do you think you're on vacation? This road has to be finished before the fall! Get to smurf!
ASSEMBLY!
?
Did you hear? An assembly!
Either we got to work or we don't-- make up your mind!
Peyo
34

My dear Smurf friends! You're wondering, no doubt, why we've smurfed you in these balls and chains? Be reassured, you're not our prisoners! Unfortunately, for all these years, you've had carefree, undisciplined lives...

It's time for you to become real Smurfs! Then you can join us!

That's well smurfed!

**BONK**

♪

Then we will smurf but one nation and we'll be--

*INVINCIBLE!*

BZzzzzz

You'd better applaud! Applaud, or else I'll--

?

*SWOOSH*

**BONK**

TCHAK

CLAP CLAP
CLAP CLAP
CLAP CLAP
CLAP
CLAP CLAP
CLAP CLAP

You're mocking us! All right then! Smurf them only stale bread and water!

Move out! Hurry up! Back to the camp!

Working or being locked up in this camp: they're really smurfing us like slaves!

At least when we're here they remove our ball and chains!

Work, always work! I can't go on! I've got to get out of here!

Poc

I'm going to smurf a very, very long tunnel and, once I get out, I'll be free! Heh heh heh!

Poor Smurf! The work is playing with his smurf!

If this goes on, we'll all end up like him!

Look at Papa Smurf! Ever since we got smurfed, he sits there all despondent!

Nok! Nok!

I'm going to have a word with him!

Papa Smurf, what's going on? Ordinarily, you'd be the last one to give up! React! We must smurf something!

!

36

Alas, my little Smurfs, there's nothing to be smurfed! Sit down, I'll tell you everything!

40

"You'll remember that, not long ago, you'd become selfish, irritable, and feisty...

"So much so you wouldn't even listen to me, your Papa Smurf...

"We were headed for a catastrophe. That's when I decided to smurf you a good lesson...

"I remembered a very complicated spell of magic that would do the job...

"After a long night of work in my laboratory, I went into the forest...

"There, in a clearing not far from our home, by the dawn's early light, I scattered a magic potion...

"...and made another village appear...

" This one was populated by belligerent Smurfs who embodied all the bad parts of each of us..."

I wanted for you, by meeting them, to become conscious of what you might become...

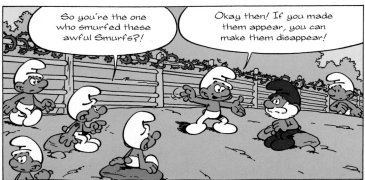
So you're the one who smurfed these awful Smurfs?!

Okay then! If you made them appear, you can make them disappear!

Yes, I could have! Unfortunately, I can't any longer!

?

37

41

"It's because all my spell books were smurfed during the attack on our village..."

Then, all is lost?!

Alas, yes! I'm afraid so!

Unless-- Papa Smurf, if I undersmurfed right, this village is the same as ours.

Exactly!

Then, there should be a laboratory like ours! And in that laboratory, lots of grimoires exsmurfly identical to yours!

Hmm! I see where you're going, Jokey Smurf!

Although the right grimoire would have to be there, the Gray Smurfs may have already smurfed it in a fire!

You never know, Papa Smurf! We have to try!

You're right, but how do we find out where the laboratory is... If it exists?!

Smurf that to me! I have an idea!

Hey, ‡psstt!‡ Is it true what they're saying in the camp? It seems you Gray Smurfs are really stupid!

WHAT? Who dares smurf that? And why?

Well, they say you don't even have a laboratory!

Of course we have one! It's the old, abandoned house over there, in the back of the village!

But we're not allowed to smurf there. Nor even to talk to you about it! So, move along now!

Well smurfed, Jokey Smurf!

I've confirmed it! They truly are very stupid!

38

Here's my plan. Hefty Smurf, Jokey Smurf, tonight, you'll smurf with me and smurf *the smurf smurfing and... the smurf smurfing are.*

Eh? What are you smurfing about? Disperse!

Heh heh! Soon, thanks to this tunnel, I'll be free! I'll smurf however long it takes, but I'll be free and won't have to work anymore!

That night, everyone is asleep in the camp...

Z

Well, almost...

Be quiet about it, Hefty Smurf!

I hope it'll catch ahold of something...

By the way, Jokey Smurf, where did you smurf this rope?

Well, I borrowed the pants from a few Smurfs and smurfed them together from end to end!

I hope they won't take long... It's starting to get cold!

BRRRR BRR

BRRR

BRR BRR

Once you're on the other side, you'll tell us if we can smurf!

It's all clear. You can smurf!

Hurry up!

?

What if we run into some Gray Smurfs?

39

Smurf some dust on your clothes! We'll pass for some of them!

Now, smurf me silently!

An isolated building. That must be it.

For smurf's sake! What a mess!

Let's not waste time! That grimoire will be hard to find! Smurf me all the books you see!

In any case, here are some ingredients already that'll be useful to smurf the potion!

BADABOOM

!

Make less noise! We'll get smurfed by a patrol!

Sorry, Papa Smurf! I-- I meant to smurf a book, and everything smurfed down on me!

?

Good fortune is coming our way! Here's the spell book I needed!

?

!

Not a moment to waste! I must smurf the potion as fast as I can!

40

And Papa Smurf worked through the night...

And there! The magic powder is ready! We just have to smurf it by the first light of day!

Just in time! Morning will dawn soon. Let's smurf back to the camp!

The road's clear, let's go!

HALT! WHO GOES THERE?!

Careful, let's do like them. Smurf your teeth!

Ah! It's you, Great Leader! I didn't recognize you!

It's working!

No problem! I was just smurfing an inspection tour!

You're dismissed now!

You silly cow!

SOUND THE ALARM! IT'S THE INTRUDERS! THEY'RE TRYING TO ESCAPE! SMURF THEM!

Oops!

41

POW BAM BOOM

Ouch!

Oww!

March! The Great Leader will decide your fate!

‡Gulp!‡ Sorry, Papa Smurf. I couldn't help myself! I'm a jokester...!

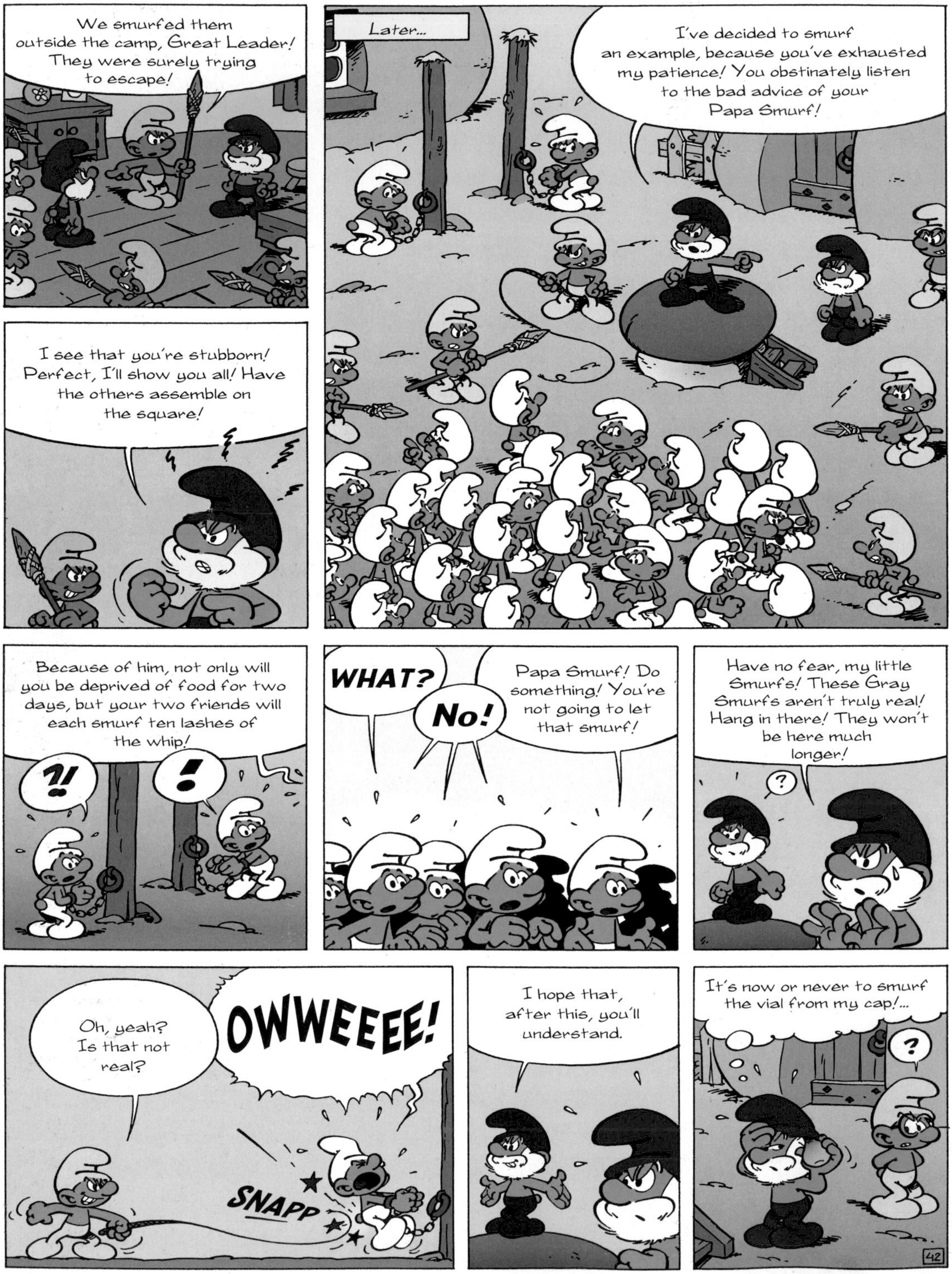

We smurfed them outside the camp, Great Leader! They were surely trying to escape!
Later...
I've decided to smurf an example, because you've exhausted my patience! You obstinately listen to the bad advice of your Papa Smurf!
I see that you're stubborn! Perfect, I'll show you all! Have the others assemble on the square!
Because of him, not only will you be deprived of food for two days, but your two friends will each smurf ten lashes of the whip!
?!
!
WHAT?
No!
Papa Smurf! Do something! You're not going to let that smurf!
Have no fear, my little Smurfs! These Gray Smurfs aren't truly real! Hang in there! They won't be here much longer!
?
Oh, yeah? Is that not real?
OWWEEEE!
SNAPP
I hope that, after this, you'll understand.
It's now or never to smurf the vial from my cap!...
?
42

Look out! The old Smurf's getting ready to smurf something!

Capture him and stop him from smurfing that bottle!

For smurf's sake! It won't open!

Smurf this vial, my little Smurfs, and open it, or else we're doomed!

Hup! Too late! I'm the one who has it! Heh heh heh!

Nobody smurf!

Well done! Smurf it to me and, above all, don't open it! It must be some devilry to smurf us!

Heh heh heh! I'm the one who saved our village! I'm a hero! I'll be the Great Leader's favorite and maybe, one day, I'll take his place and--

Hee hee! There! A souvenir from Jokey Smurf!

!

Curses! The vial has been smurfed!

Uh-oh...

What's going on? I feel all smurfy...

Look! The Gray Smurfs! They're becoming transparent!

43

47

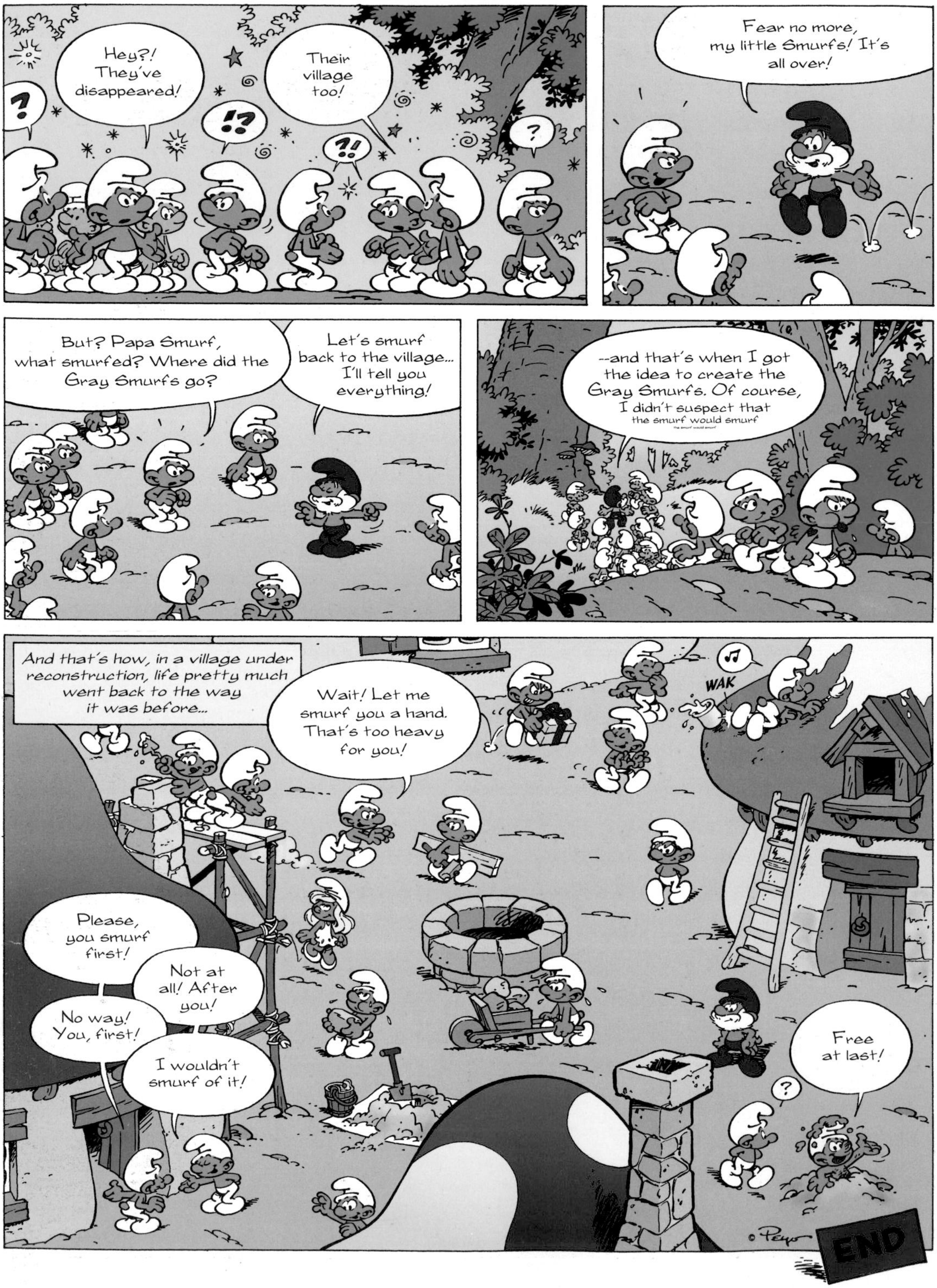
?
Hey?! They've disappeared!
!?
?!
Their village too!
?
Fear no more, my little Smurfs! It's all over!
But? Papa Smurf, what smurfed? Where did the Gray Smurfs go?
Let's smurf back to the village... I'll tell you everything!
--and that's when I got the idea to create the Gray Smurfs. Of course, I didn't suspect that
the smurf would smurf
And that's how, in a village under reconstruction, life pretty much went back to the way it was before...
Wait! Let me smurf you a hand. That's too heavy for you!
WAK
Please, you smurf first!
Not at all! After you!
No way! You, first!
I wouldn't smurf of it!
?
Free at last!
© Peyo
END

# THE SHADOW OF THE SMURF APPRENTICE

Okay! Okay! Since you insist, Apprentice Smurf, I authorize you to smurf a few little experiments! You can use all the ingredients here...

...On the other hand, don't smurf these bottles here! Their contents are smurfly dangerous!

I must go away for a moment! Be very careful!

I promise, Papa Smurf!

And now, quickly, some experiments! Magic experiments!

Hmm! Okay, I have to find what I need! I need a sandglass!

Ah! I'll smurf this one!

NOK

OOPS!

BAM BENG

⸱Whew!⸱ Luckily, it's not broken! I'll smurf it back in its place!

But the Apprentice Smurf didn't realize that part of the phial's contents had spread over **HIS SHADOW!**

Peyo

49

Soon after... And to finish off, a smurf of morning dew...

...I hope it'll smurf!

A BLUE ROSE, *YIPPEE!* It smurfed!

I have to go smurf Papa Smurf about this!

So, Apprentice Smurf? Has Papa Smurf finally let you smurf some experiments?

Yes, yes! I just smurfed one, and it worked!

But the Apprentice Smurf doesn't see his shadow has come to life and is playing a bad trick on Painter Smurf!

HEY!

No way! Are you out of your smurf?!

Hello, Smurfette, have you seen Papa Smurf? Yes! He just smurfed in front of my window! He can't be far!

?

CRAK!

OOOH! What a jerk! He knocked over my beautiful flowers and didn't even smurf!

2

Unbeknownst to all, the Apprentice Smurf's shadow is continuing its bad jokes...

My eggs!

≡WAAAAH!≡ My mirror!

Now, that's enough! I've had it!

Hey, Apprentice Smurf! Have you gone completely smurfers? You're going to fix everything you've smurfed right now!

?

But--but it's not me! I didn't do anything!

Oh, no? Who was it then?

What's going on here?

It's the Apprentice Smurf, Papa Smurf! He's having fun smurfing all of our stuff!

But it's not true!

Come now, Apprentice Smurf, it really wasn't you who smurfed all that?

Of course not, Papa Smurf!

Suddenly, the shadow slips behind Papa Smurf and...

?

OWW!

But--

?!

OH! His shadow! That's what smurfed you, Papa Smurf!

My shadow?

?

?

?

LOOK OUT! It's smurfing away!

STOP! You can't get by!

POW

My shadow, quick! Smurf it!

BONK

We'll never manage to smurf it, Papa Smurf!

It smurfed right through the mesh of my net!

Wait! It's my shadow. I'll smurf it!

POW

There! I got it!

Well smurfed!

POW OUCH!

Too late! It's smurfed away!

Apprentice Smurf, you smurfed into the dangerous substances I'd told you not to smurf!

Yes, Papa Smurf, but it was an accident, and now I've smurfed my shadow, ⸫ sniff!⸫

Okay! This isn't too serious! I'll smurf a solution in my spell books!

Oh! Thank you, Papa Smurf!

That evening, Papa Smurf read through a few, very interesting books!

*Yaawn!* That's enough for today! It's time to go to smurf!

What? There's a light still in my laboratory?

I thought I'd smurfed it out!

Nobody's here! And that spell book wasn't open earlier!

"How to Bring Shadows to Life"?!

Apprentice Smurf must be wanting to smurf something! But what--?

Apprentice Smurf! Are you the one who smurfed into my laboratory this evening?

Me, Papa Smurf? No! I smurfed to bed early tonight!

?

Hmm? But who could have wanted to smurf that formula?

Good smurf, but of course! Your shadow! That's what's in my laboratory!

It's trying its best to smurf life to our shadows!

We absolutely must stop it! But you alone can smurf it!

Listen closely, I have a plan! We'll try to smurf your shadow at your place! And then, you'll bzzzzzzzz...

A little later...
SO, APPRENTICE SMURF, YOU'D LIKE TO SMURF MY SPELL BOOK TO YOUR HOME TO READ?

YES, PAPA SMURF! IT'D SMURF ME REALLY HAPPY TO SMURF IT HOME!

OKAY, THEN, BUT TAKE GOOD CARE OF IT!

YOU CAN SMURF ON ME, PAPA SMURF!

♪Yawwwn!♪ I'm tired! I'm going to smurf!

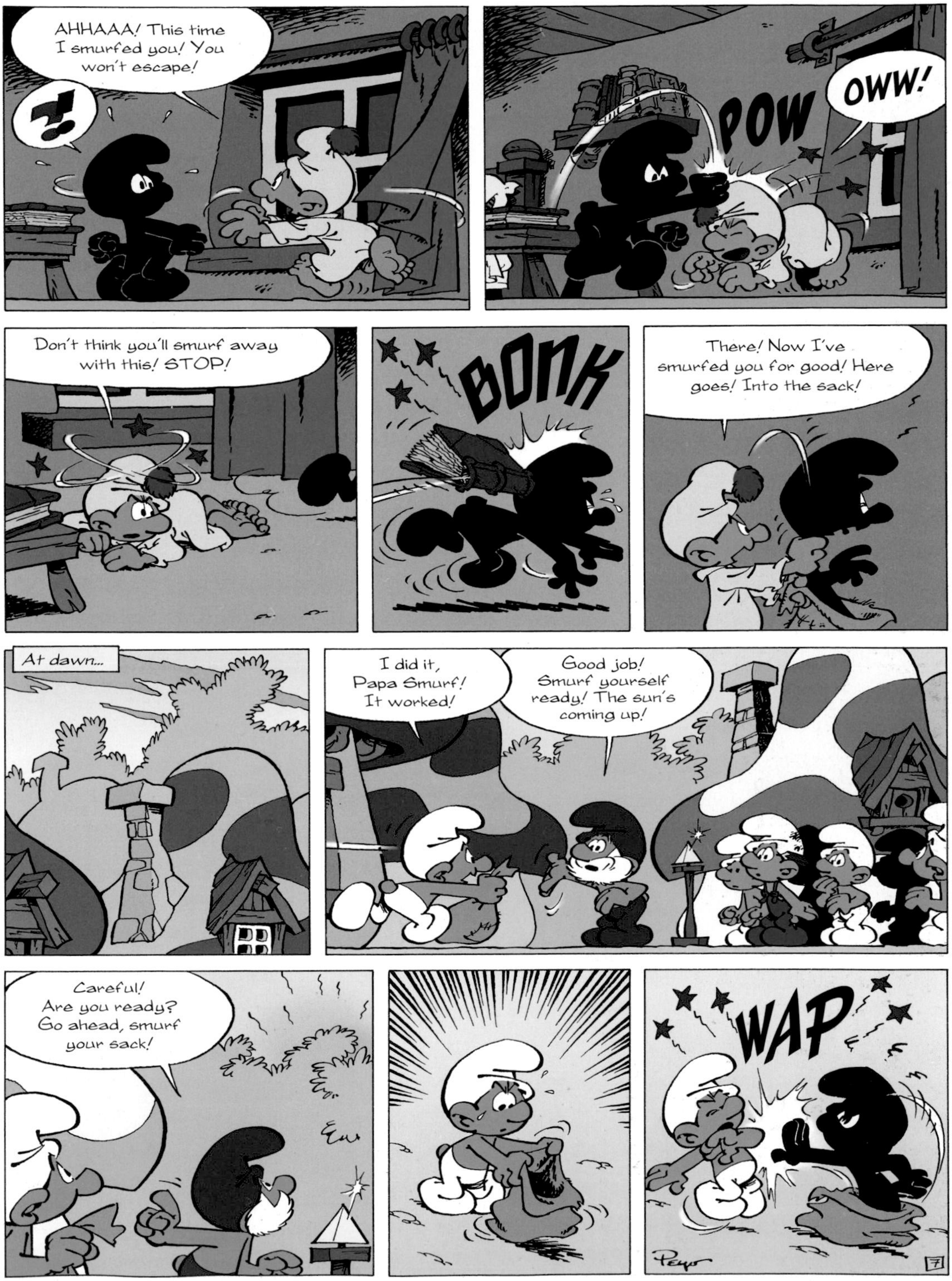
AHHAAA! This time I smurfed you! You won't escape!
!
POW
OWW!
Don't think you'll smurf away with this! STOP!
BONK
There! Now I've smurfed you for good! Here goes! Into the sack!
At dawn...
I did it, Papa Smurf! It worked!
Good job! Smurf yourself ready! The sun's coming up!
Careful! Are you ready? Go ahead, smurf your sack!
WAP
Peyo
7

Quick! Aim the prism so the sunbeams smurf on the shadow!

?

It feels itself being inexorably drawn by the beam...

?!

...until it's completely absorbed!

Quick, smurf onto your shadow!

You did it, Papa Smurf! It smurfs like me! I'm smurfed!

Let that smurf you a lesson, Apprentice Smurf! Be more careful next time!

I promise, Papa Smurf!

Hey, there! Careful! Don't smurf on my shadow! Now that I have it!

The next day...

HELP!

?

Look! My shadow! It has come to life, too!

!!

Papa Smurf! Papa Smurf! Come quick! It's a catasmurfre!

Hee hee hee! Thanks, Painter Smurf!

That was a good one, Jokey Smurf!

END

# THE MANSION OF A THOUSAND MIRRORS

This day, like all the others, Vanity Smurf was admiring himself...

I am so handsome!

Really handsome!

Really, really handsome!

Thanks, Smurfette!

It's really very smurf of you to do the cleaning. My laboratory needed it!

It's my pleasure, Papa Smurf!

This armoire is locked. Do you have the key?

**NO!** NOT THAT ONE! THAT ARMOIRE MUST REMAIN SHUT!

Here's where I smurf the most dangerous formulas and my greatest secrets!

Oh?

And in particular, the map that leads to the Mansion of a Thousand Mirrors...

*A MANSION OF A THOUSAND MIRRORS?!*

You understand why I can't smurf the key to you--despite all the trust I smurf in you!

Fine, whatever! That piece will stay dirty, that's all!

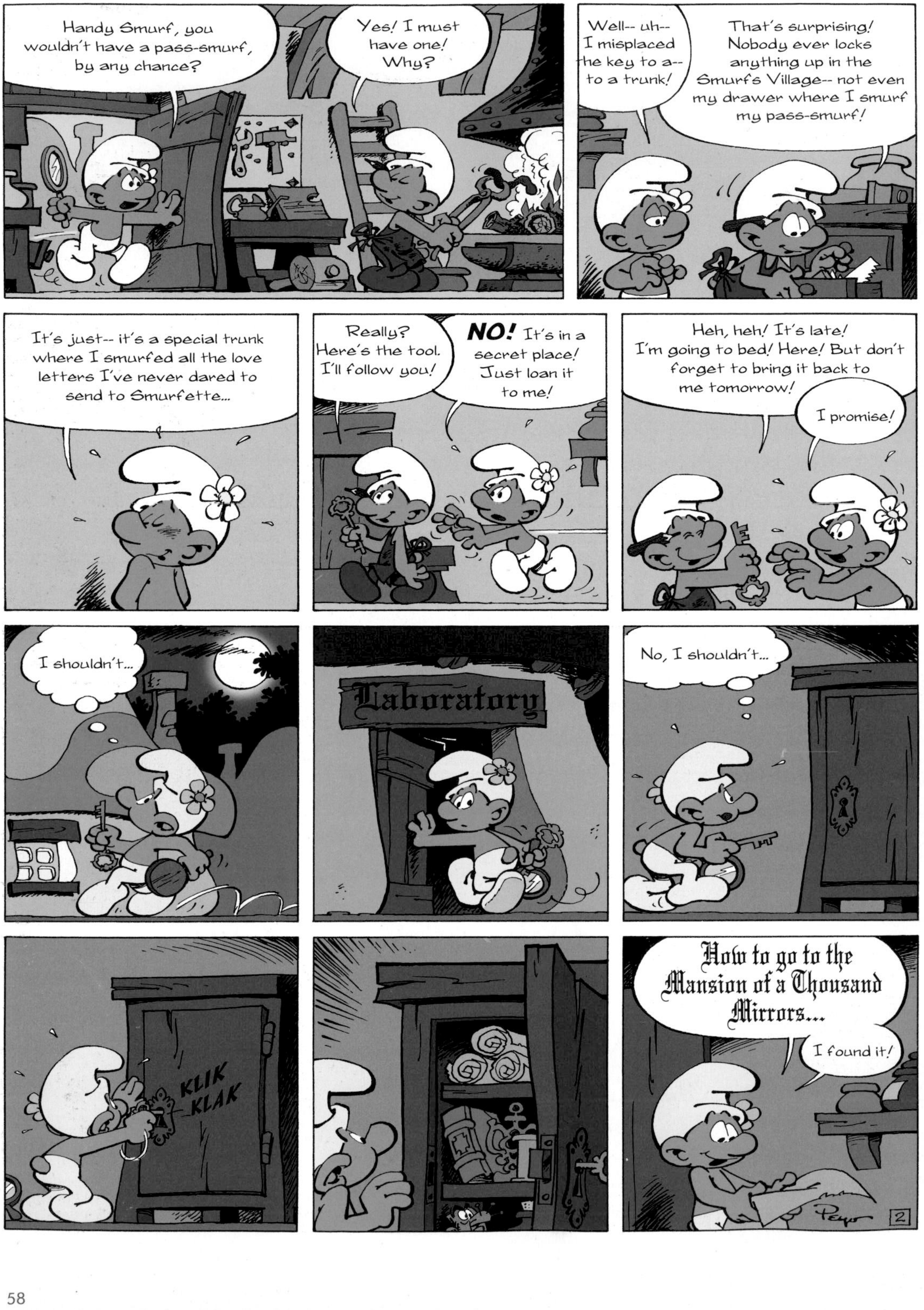
Handy Smurf, you wouldn't have a pass-smurf, by any chance?
Yes! I must have one! Why?
Well-- uh-- I misplaced the key to a-- to a trunk!
That's surprising! Nobody ever locks anything up in the Smurfs Village-- not even my drawer where I smurf my pass-smurf!
It's just-- it's a special trunk where I smurfed all the love letters I've never dared to send to Smurfette...
Really? Here's the tool. I'll follow you!
NO! It's in a secret place! Just loan it to me!
Heh, heh! It's late! I'm going to bed! Here! But don't forget to bring it back to me tomorrow!
I promise!
I shouldn't...
Laboratory
No, I shouldn't...
KLIK KLAK
How to go to the Mansion of a Thousand Mirrors...
I found it!
Peyo
2

...turn left at the third thicket of pine trees, then smurf in front of a big oak-tree...

...cross a ford and smurf straight ahead...

According to the map, it's just behind this embankment.

There it is!

You don't go into a mansion of a thousand mirrors with a little hand-smurf!

!

Peyo

3

It's fantastic with all these mirrors!

And it's crazy how handsome I am!

I never get tired of it!

A true marvel!

But Vanity Smurf doesn't realize his reflections are staying in the mirrors...

This is the most smurftastic night of my life!

Oh! A funhouse mirror! I don't like this one!

There's even one on the ceiling!

This is all very lovely, but I have to smurf back to the village before dawn!

What a beautiful mansion! I don't understand why Papa Smurf doesn't want us to know about it.

Is he gone?

Yes! Let's follow him!

I'm so handsome!

And me, too!

4

60

We're so handsome!

Very handsome!

We may only be reflections, but what handsome reflections!

Yeah!

Ah! The Smurf Village! Quick! I have to resmurf the map to the laboratory!

KLIK KLAK

And there! That was a nice, beautiful adventure! Now, I'm going to bed

Oh, Vanity Smurf! Don't forget to give me back my pass-smurf!

What pass-smurf?

Well, I never! What a scoundrel!

Hey, here's the pass-smurf you loaned to me!

Your portrait? But you keep asking for them!

More flowers! But that's the thirteenth bouquet you've brought me, Vanity Smurf!

Peyo

5

A little later...

Ah, I slept great!

I get it. I'm still asleep. I'll go back to bed!

Say, Vanity Smurf, have you read my new book of proverbs?

Oh! Sorry!

I need to smurf off my glasses!

Hello, Papa Smurf!

Hello, Papa Smurf!

Hello, Vanity Smurfs!

Me, I don't like all these Vanity Smurfs!

Something strange is going on. Where's Vanity Smurf?

÷OOF!÷

Hey! Vanity Smurf! Come look out the window!

You haven't gone to the mansion of a thousand mirrors, by any chance?

Uh... Well, yes!

You poor fool! All your reflections followed you back here!

But the worst part is that you yourself are disappearing! Look, your colors are already starting to fade!

It's horrible! We have to smurf something!

Quick! To the laboratory!

Where did I put that tuning fork? Ah! There it is! And the map that leads to the mansion...

Vanity Smurfs! Follow me!

Laboratory

Papa Smurf! I'm becoming transparent!

Fast! Faster!

We're finally there!

Vanities, you come in with us! You others, wait out here!

Reflections, all of you back into your mirrors! Get hopping!

Papa Smurf! I've almost disappeared entirely!

I'm going to go see what they're doing.

Quick! The tuning fork!

CRRR OOOIIIIINNNGG CRRRR ZZZOOD CRRR

YIPPEE! I've resmurfed!

KRESH

Well?

It's okay! Everything's back in order! Let's smurf back to the village!

Why are you so sad, Vanity Smurf?

My hand-mirror broke, too! It's sad, but I'm so handsome!

Your glasses? Broken? Ah! Papa Smurf always says "curiosity kills the cat" and--

8 END